THE SOLSTICE'S BRIDE

THE SOLSTICE'S BRIDE

A Prequel to the Cursed Queens Series

E. E. HORNBURG

E.E. Hornburg Books

For all of those who love snowy days, hot chocolate, and celebrating
the season with those who matter most.

Contents

Map

THE KNOWN KINGDOMS
TOWN OF SLANIA
KINGDOM OF GRESIN
CITY OF MARALIS
LUANA'S CASTLE
PARAVIAN MOUNTAINS
THE DRAVIAN ISLANDS
COLMA HIGH TEMPLE
GRANDMOTHER'S COTTAGE
FARREN CITY
LYARE HIGH TEMPLE
KINGDOM OF MARALI
TULLI LAKE
THE LOTUS RIVER
TEMPLE LAKE
GALLIS HIGH TEMPLE
KINGDOM OF IMARE
KINGDOM OF OXARE
KINGDOM OF OYAE
KAHDI DESERT
CITY OF OYAE
BELOVIAN ISLANDS
ISLA HIGH TEMPLE
TO UNCHARTED WESTERN SEA
THE CEPYRA SEA

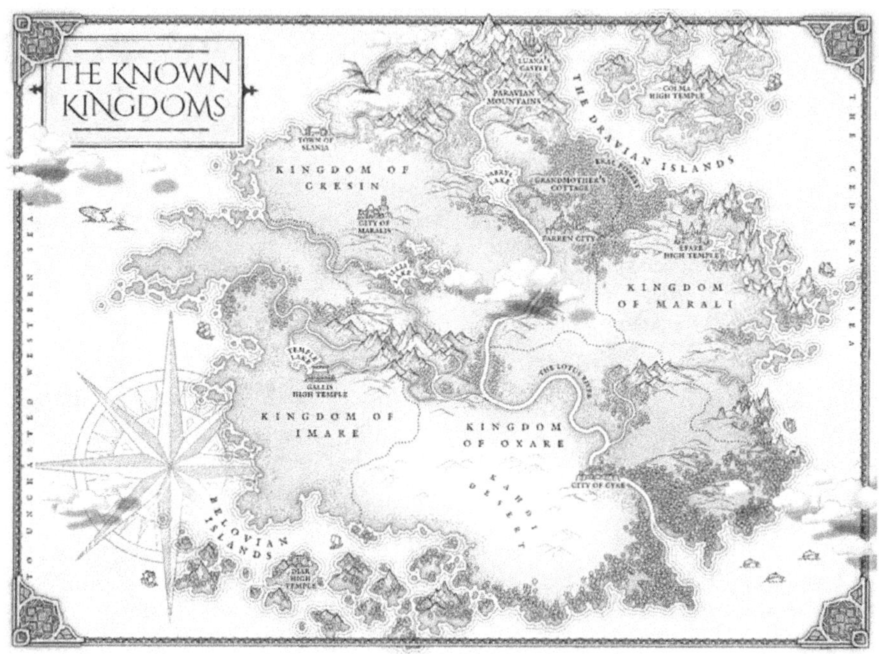

I

This was a stupid idea, Lennox thought for the millionth time as she trudged along toward Farren Castle and clutched the red cloak around her. It hadn't been snowing flakes the size of rocks when she left Eral Forest, but it was too late to turn back now. Besides, there was no way she was returning to Mama after the argument they'd had, even if it was only a couple of days before the Winter Solstice.

The faint silhouette of the castle came into view when she was nearly on top of it. Usually, she could see it from the edge of the forest. Tonight, the storm made it practically invisible.

Lennox straightened her shoulders and did her best to make herself not appear so pathetic as she approached the gates. She may need them to give her shelter, but it didn't mean she had no pride.

"Right this way!" A man stood at the castle gate dressed in a fur-lined cloak and waved Lennox over. The shiny silver fabric and buttons of his tunic glistened beneath the star lantern in his hand, making him a beacon of light in the storm.

Lennox gathered her energy and hurried toward him, though it felt as though her legs were about to collapse beneath her. He lifted the lantern, so it illuminated his face and she almost gasped.

He had the brightest blue eyes she'd ever seen, so bright she almost didn't notice the crescent moon tattooed on his forehead. *A follower of Luana, goddess of the moon and winter.* With the magic from his goddess, he probably enjoyed this sort of weather.

Those blue eyes roamed over her face and body, and for a moment when he smiled, it was as though the storm vanished. She should have felt self-conscious, but found herself smiling back. There was something oddly familiar about him.

"Hello there," he purred and it warmed Lennox all the way down to her snow-soaked toes.

"Hello," she managed to croak. It sounded as though the cold had frozen her voice.

"You came just in time; we were about to close the doors. Most everyone else has already had at least a pint by now. But don't worry, we have plenty."

Everyone else? Lennox opened and closed her mouth as she thought of a response. It was as though he'd been expecting her.

The starlight from the lamp glistened and danced over the snow as he led the way to the castle. Two guards opened the doors for them and bowed their heads. Lennox hurried to follow him into the warmth of the indoors.

"Everyone else?" She asked once they were inside.

"For the Peasants Ball of course!"

Lennox bristled as a servant took her cloak to be hung and dried. *Peasants Ball?* She may have been cold and wet, and her lifestyle in Eral Forest may not have been as luxurious as one who lived in a castle, but *peasant?*

"Excuse me?" The stunned shyness she'd had when she first saw the man vanished.

"And don't worry about your clothes. We'll find something warmer and finer for you to wear." He gestured to another servant who bowed and rushed off to retrieve whatever it was the single hand gesture meant. "As you are the last to arrive, you won't have as much of a variety to pick from, but I'm sure you'll find something to your liking. We have more than enough to go around."

Lennox pushed her sleeve up to reveal the tattoo of a stag formed of twigs and roses and extended to him. Being part fae, she didn't need a tattoo like most people did to use magic, but it did make it stronger. "Don't you know who I am?"

He smirked in amusement, not paying her tattoo any mind. "No, as you never introduced yourself. What is your name my fine lady?"

She straightened her stance, her green eyes meeting his blue ones. "Lennox, daughter of Renata, Kutlaous' Minister."

The man tilted his head to the side and circled around Lennox as though he were inspecting a new horse to purchase for the royal stables. Some sight she must have been to him with wet and tangled red hair and her fur-lined green tunic and tight pants clinging to her like she was a wet dog. "Huh. I'd think one dedicated to the god of nature would be able to withstand the elements a bit better."

"To an extent. The conditions are a bit more extreme than usual." She hated how she felt the need to defend herself to this guard. "Now, if you please, I request an audience with the royal family. I am in need of their assistance."

"Are you coming to the ball or not, Brennan? What in Luana's name is taking so long?" A tall woman in a blue ballgown stormed into the entryway. The bite in her voice had the same effect as the harsh wind outside and sent a shiver down Lennox's spine. The starry crown on her raven hair glimmered against the blue tapestries in the lamp light as the servants bowed.

*Brennan? Wasn't that the name of...*The man smiled at the crowned woman and after a quick bow gave her a peck on the cheek. "Perfect timing, Mother. It seems as though the daughter of Kutlaus' Minister has decided to join us for the Peasants Ball."

The crowned prince of Cresin.

Well, damn it all to Stula's realm. No wonder he looked familiar.

The queen raised a brow and looked Lennox over head to foot. "Is she now? She looks like a rat. I'd have thought a follower of Kutlaus would be able to withstand the elements better. Especially if she's Renata's daughter."

Did they all have to harp on that?

"The only one who could possibly come out unscathed in this

storm is Luana herself," Lennox snapped, but paused as the queen's eyes widened. Lennox cleared her throat and dipped into a curtsey. "My apologies, your majesty. I seem to have forgotten myself as I'm still cold from the storm, which I'm sure you can see."

Considering her wet clothes clung to her like a second skin, Lennox was sure everyone could see *everything* she was feeling.

The queen pursed her lips and only offered a small "hm" as a response. She waved her hand for Lennox to stand upright again. "Daughter of Renata come to join the Peasant's Ball?"

From the tone in the queen's voice, Lennox could tell she didn't believe her for a moment.

"I've come to see you, actually, your majesty. I request your assistance."

Lips still pursed; the queen sighed. "Get her in some proper clothes and have her come to us once she's presentable. Brennan, I expect you in the ball room presently."

With that, the queen turned on her heel and made her exit.

Prince Brennan stood in front of Lennox, his arms crossed in front of his broad chest with a bemused smile. She wanted to slap that amusement off his face, no matter how handsome it was. "It seems you got your request for an audience with the royal family."

2

Windows so large they took up the entirety of the walls created the illusion of being in the snow beneath the night sky. Boughs of pine branches and wreaths frosted in stardust hung over each one, as well as across the ceiling of the ballroom.

A servant carrying a tray of copper mugs garnished with cinnamon sticks offered her one. As she sipped the cider, it warmed her all the way to her toes. Whatever liquor they'd spiked it with would make her head spin by the end of the night if she wasn't careful.

Lennox pushed her way towards the back of the room where the king and queen sat perched on their silver thrones. Prince Brennan caught her eye, and he smiled. A genuine one, not like the smirks and sly glances when they first met. What a fool he must have thought her for not realizing he was the prince. She wanted to kick herself for not recognizing him sooner. It wasn't as though he recognized her at first either – even if she wasn't as recognizable. In spite of it all, she couldn't help but enjoy his admiring gaze.

The queen, however, had not changed her expression and maintained pursed lips as Lennox curtsied before her. At least the king offered a warm smile.

"It has been many years since we've had the pleasure of hosting a Minister of Kutlaous," he said when she stood again.

"The Minister is my mother, Renata," Lennox clarified. "She did not join me tonight, though I'm sure she sends her warmest regards."

Maybe.

As Minister, Mother was the god Kutlaous' representative in his stead, so she was bound to Eral Forest. The few instances she left were short periods of time before she was beckoned back. Mother preferred it that way. As much as Lennox loved Eral, she did not feel the same.

"So, she claims," the queen said, ice in her voice. "We have no evidence she is who she says. It has been many years since we've seen the Minister or her daughter. This could be anyone coming in asking for our help."

Lennox extended her arm to show her dress off, and as she summoned the earth magic flowing through her veins, the tattoo glowed. All the silver coated poinsettias filling the room sparkled a bright and sparkling red.

She couldn't help but swell with pride when Prince Brennan's smile grew wider, and a hint of realization shone in his blue eyes.

"A parlor trick. Any follower of Kutlaous could have done the same," the queen said with a sigh.

The king leaned over and patted his wife's hand. "Let the girl speak. If I remember correctly, she has many of the features of Renata's daughter." He then faced Lennox. "What is it you request of us?"

A wave of relief washed through her as Lennox curtsied to him. At least one of them was willing to give her a chance. "Thank you, your majesty. It's the ogres you see."

Those around them who were in ear shot gasped and twittered like a nest of birds whose tree had just been shaken.

"If you are bringing the ogres here..." the queen started.

Lennox interrupted her. "They have no interest in any life outside of Eral Forest, which is why this was the perfect place for me to come. But they do want more power in Eral, and their most prominent clan has threatened my mother and I. Unless I marry one of them, they will take both our home and myself by force."

Silence fell over them after her announcement. Lennox swallowed the lump in her throat and held her breath as the king and queen considered her.

"While we are sorry for your troubles, if you are who you say, what are we supposed to do?" The queen asked. "Surely, Renata has some way to seek help from your god."

"We have reinforced our protections around the cottage, and we've recruited fae to stand guard. But we cannot hide forever or ban those who need us. Each time I leave home, the ogres attempt to kidnap me. I only seek shelter here for a few days. If the ogres see we have allied ourselves with Cresin, we can calm them. I am favored to be the next Minister, and your goodness will not be forgotten when I take my place."

The king stroked his graying beard and took in a deep breath. "And you swear the ogres will not come here if we shelter you?"

Lennox nodded. "They hate everything about civilized society. They would never be caught in a city, let alone a castle."

"Very well. Enjoy the ball while we consider your request. We will not send you back out into the storm and will let you know our answer by morning."

Lennox sighed and curtsied again. At least it was progress, if a temporary solution. "Thank you, your majesties."

Dismissed, Lennox joined the rest of the night's revelers. She'd heard about the grand and lavish celebrations Farren Castle held for the solstice. How for days they held balls and parties and ceremonies and stayed up until dawn, basking in the longest time of darkness of the year when the moon goddess, Luana, ruled the sky. Although the details of the celebrations she wasn't sure of.

Prince Brennan extended his hand to Lennox. "Dance with me?"

Her eyes met his blue ones, and she attempted to calm her warming cheeks. "It would be my pleasure, your highness."

He pulled her into his arms, and they spun around the dance floor. The prince had stunning eyes and shaggy black hair she wanted to run her fingers through. There was something about him she couldn't help but be drawn to, and she reveled being so close to him.

"What is this ball about?" Lennox managed to ask once she'd gotten her head together.

"The Peasants' Ball," Prince Brennan answered. "It's for the people of Farren, and we host it each year before the Solstice."

"Thus, why you called me a peasant when I arrived."

"You were pretty ragged."

She had to give him that. Even on a usual day she didn't look much like the nobles he was most likely used to with her simple tunics and pants.

"It's a charity event for those below you," she said, testing his response.

The sparkle in his eyes dimmed. "Yes and no. We offer clothing they normally would not have, which they get to keep, warmth and shelter on one of the longest and coldest nights of the year, and food they are welcome to take home. But there's more to it than that." He turned them as they danced and pointed toward small groups speaking off to the sides. Some had heads bent in deep discussions, others shook hands, and some toasted one another. "This is their largest business building event of the year. Many of them have found employment through this ball. They dole out negotiations among each other, marriage arrangements are made, I've even heard of some people finding housing."

Some of the remaining chill from the storm thawed from Lennox's heart and she smiled up at the prince. "Although perhaps the name 'Peasants' Ball' is a bit demeaning?"

Prince Brennan chuckled. "It's tradition, and Farren loves its traditions. But perhaps we can think of something new to name it."

She raised her brows. "We?"

He pulled her in closer so their bodies pressed against each other, and she could feel his heart pounding in time with hers. He leaned in, and his lips brushed against her ear. A shiver ran through her. "I remember you."

Lennox had to catch her breath. She had been to Farren Castle once before as a young girl. A disease had spread through Eral, and Mother needed the assistance of the royal family and their Attendants to help heal the forest dwellers.

"You do?"

"It took me a moment, as it has been several years, and given the state you were in. But how could I forget that tangled red mess on your head or those dazzling green eyes? Besides, you'd told me back then what you wanted your tattoo for Kutlaous to be and I recognized the image on your arm."

So, he had recognized her, and she'd been the fool to not realize who he was. He must have been mocking her the entire time.

His voice lowered so only the two of them could hear the conversation. "I have a proposition for you, which I think will solve both of our problems."

She tilted her head to the side. "Both of our problems?"

"You should marry me."

"What?" Lennox stopped in her tracks causing him to trip over her feet and they bumped into a pair of other dancers who shot them a dirty look until they realized it was the prince, then bowed and moved on. "You want me to marry you?"

"What better way to be rid of an ogre proposal than to marry a prince? Being allied with me, we'd also be able to protect your mother."

Oddly enough, it was a more logical solution than any of the ones Lennox had come up with on her own. It made sense, if she ignored that they hardly knew each other. She would have to leave Eral Forest and walk away from her place as the future Minister.

"And what problem of yours would it solve?"

Prince Brennan grimaced at her question. "The newlywed prince of Oxare in the south, his wife has given birth to a son. His name is Alvis and will be dedicated to the sun god Ray. Which means, the people would be pleased if I settled down and were blessed with a daughter."

Realization dawned on Lennox. If Prince Brennan were to be married and have a daughter, the two babies would be Ray and Luana's Chosens. It was the greatest tradition in all of the kingdoms.

"To be the father of Luana's Chosen would be an honor," she told him.

"As it would to be the mother."

Lennox looked around the room, not letting herself meet his eyes, because if she did, she might do something ridiculous like accept. "You must be mad. Besides, I might live in Eral, but I've heard about your exploits. I'm sure one of the train of men or women who come in and out of your bedroom would be delighted to help you in your plight."

The prince was well loved in his kingdom in more ways than one if the rumors were true. No one begrudged him for it as all his partners were willing.

"Perhaps." He pulled Lennox in closer still; his blue eyes pierced through her with snow and ice magic he surely received from Luana. "But I'm drawn to you. From the moment I saw you outside. Can't you feel it, Lennox?"

Her heart pounded as he looked at her and the room around them faded away. "We barely know each other, and I'd be giving up everything, including my place as Kutlaous' next Minister."

"A role which isn't guaranteed. You must take part in the Trials first, and Kutlaous can choose anyone."

Lennox had never allowed herself to think about an alternative. Completing the Trials to become Minister had been the trajectory for her whole life. Perhaps there had been fleeting moments when she wondered what a life outside of Eral would be like, but she'd never let them linger. Something in her chest fluttered at the idea of something else she could do, somewhere else she could live, especially if it was with him...

She shook her head. It was all too fast.

"Then we'll make it temporary," Prince Brennan amended. "We'll tell everyone we're engaged for now until both of us find another solution and a way to protect you and your mother more permanently."

It would be an excellent way to deter the ogres. At least for now.

"All right."

The smile on his face was more than enough confirmation for Lennox that as outrageous as the idea was, she'd said the right thing.

3

E ngaged indeed," the queen muttered as they walked through the halls of Farren Castle when the ball ended.

The morning sun shone through the windows but did nothing to prevent Lennox from yawning. She wasn't used to parties which lasted until daybreak, and there were to be two more nights like this if she were to stay for the remainder of the solstice celebrations.

"Is it common for you to escort guests to their rooms?" Lennox asked. The king and queen were less than pleased when she and Prince Brennan told them their "plan" to get married. The one reprieve would be going to bed until the next night's events so she could have the chance to gather her thoughts.

The queen looked over her shoulder and gave Lennox the gift of a sugary-sweet smile that made her want to recoil. "Not at all. But I want to be sure my future daughter in law is comfortable and has a proper welcome to our home."

Lennox had the sinking feeling this wasn't a good thing.

They came to one of the bed chambers and the queen opened the door with a flourish as though she were showing off the crown jewels. Lennox couldn't contain her gasp at the sight inside. Before her stood a bed with mattresses stacked so high it almost reached the ceiling.

"Don't worry, it's perfectly safe." The queen smiled again with a wicked glint in her eyes. She stalked into the room with her arms crossed. "If my son wants to marry the daughter of Kutlaous' Minister, even I have to admit it's not a terrible choice. But I'm not convinced you are who you say you are. People have attempted to trick us in the past and I'm not letting just any wench with a sob story into our family. Prove to us you are who you say, and I'll consider permitting this engagement." She turned on her heel and went back to the door. "We'll see you in the afternoon."

Lennox shook her head. This was ridiculous. "How will sleeping on a pile of mattresses prove anything?"

The queen only offered a small shrug of her regal shoulder. "If I were to tell you, it would defeat the whole point, wouldn't it? Sleep well."

With that, the door clicked shut and Lennox was alone with the monstrosity of a bed.

Thankfully, a ladder had been left for her to use to climb to the top. Once Lennox changed into the softest, warmest purple nightgown she'd ever worn, she propped the ladder next to the bed and began her ascent. With each step she peered at the bed, examining it for any hint as to what she was supposed to do to prove she was Renata's daughter.

Light shone over the mattresses and Lennox paused her climbing and glanced over her shoulder to see Prince Brennan at the door. His eyes opened with shock then he burst into laughter.

"It's not funny."

"Oh, but my lady, it is." He shut the door and came further into the room and bent backwards to see to the top. "Whatever has my mother done this time?"

"Somehow this is supposed to help me prove I am who I say. And what are you doing here? Shouldn't you be in your own room?"

A mischievous glint appeared in his bright blue eyes, making Lennox's stomach flip. "How are people to believe we are engaged if I don't bother to stay in the same room as my betrothed? It would be highly out of character for me, and no one would believe our ruse."

Lennox huffed out a laugh, in spite of the heat rising in her. "I am not bedding you."

Even so, she couldn't help but imagine what his lips and hands on her would feel like; what those eyes would look like as they gazed at her body while he was on top of her... no. She shook the thoughts from her head.

"You don't have to. We only need to make others believe we can't bear to be away from one another for even a day. Besides, perhaps between the two of us we can figure out what my mother's ridiculous scheme is."

Lennox glanced at the mattresses then back to him and sighed. "Fine. I'm too exhausted to argue and it looks as though there is enough room for the two of us to sleep without bothering one another."

"Unless you want to of course."

Lennox tightened her grasp on the rungs of the ladder and took in a deep breath. This was going to be a long night. Or day, rather.

He followed after her and they each slid under the fur lined blue quilt with enough space for a wolf to take a nap between them. He'd removed his purple robe, leaving his chest bare, and it took everything in Lennox to not gape at the muscles revealed to her. She bit her lip and flopped onto her back to stare at the ceiling.

They lay side by side for what felt like an eternity. How could he be so relaxed when her heart raced this way? She turned onto her side and gazed at his profile. His black curls seemed so soft against the silk pillows. She wanted to reach out and run her fingers through them.

"I feel you staring."

Thankfully, the thick curtains blocked out the morning sun so it was dark, and he couldn't see her face flush. "Sorry. I'm not used to sharing a bed."

"Really?" He turned onto his side, so he faced her. "You've never shared a bed with anyone?"

"I have. But not often. At least not to sleep." She wasn't an inexperienced maiden by any means.

Prince Brennan chuckled and it rumbled the sheets. "Understood."

"Out of all the people you know from court, why would you want to marry me?" The question had danced on her tongue all night. While the temporary solution was helpful, his motivations still didn't make sense.

"Other than the excellent alliance, and how lovely you are?"

There went the flushing face again. Why did he have to be so charming? "Yes, other than that."

"I don't want my spouse to be picked out for me, as I'm sure you don't either. Women have been paraded in front of me my whole life, and they're fine. If it wasn't for needing to have an heir, I'm sure men would be paraded in front of me too. But I want someone exciting. I don't have many choices of my own, but that's one thing I may have some control over. You're someone I could picture keeping life interesting."

Not the answer she was expecting. Not that she was sure what he would say. Something still didn't seem right though. "What about your supposed future daughter?"

Brennan propped his head in his hand. "What do you mean?"

"If you have a daughter as your firstborn, she will have to marry the prince of Oxare because they'll be the Chosens of Luana and Ray. You would be telling her who to marry; the very thing you want to avoid."

"It's different. As the Chosens, they're the expression of Luana and Ray's love for each other here in our world, the way the god and goddess can be together. They're destined."

The tradition went back to when the kingdoms of Cresin and Oxare were at war with one another, and Queen Isadore and King Sanson married, claiming they were Chosen by the god and goddess. The war had little to do with Eral Forest, where Lennox lived.

"I suppose."

Brennan sat up and leaned against the headboard; his hand almost brushed hers in the process. "Don't you believe in destiny?"

She followed this lead and sat facing him, her legs crossed under her. "I think we make our own destiny."

A tiny sliver of light crossed over the prince's handsome face. It was enough to show off the sly smile on those lips Lennox couldn't get her mind off of. "Don't tell the people of Cresin that. They'd be shocked to their core."

"They do love their traditions in Cresin."

"That they do."

4

Lennox woke in the late afternoon to find she was alone. Her treck through the snowstorm and dancing all night had left her exhausted, but in spite of it she found herself waking periodically because she couldn't help but marvel at having the crowned prince in her bed.

There certainly had been enough room, and Prince Brennan kept a healthy distance between them, as promised. She knew she should have been glad but couldn't help wonder what it would have been like to fall asleep in his arms.

With a sigh, she made the journey to the ground and circled around the bed. If the purpose of the mattresses had something to do with proving who she was, there had to be something about this bed which called to her magic.

Lennox closed her eyes and under her breath sang a tune of Eral Forest. Even from beneath the fleece sleeves of the nightgown her tattoo glowed, and swirls of green magic danced out from her fingertips. The spirit of the earth flowed through her veins and hummed beneath her skin. There was definitely something in the room, but she couldn't tell what it was.

A knock came at the door and interrupted her thoughts, leaving no time to decipher it. It was time to go pretend to be in love with a prince. Something she found easier than originally anticipated.

***

Outside, Lennox gathered along with all the nobles who'd arrived through the day. They faced the hills and snow, the outline of Eral Forest's entrance a faint shadow in the distance.

Lennox's chest tightened. What was Mama doing now? Was she worried about her? Or worse- had the ogres heard of her running away and Mama was paying the price?

"There's my lovely finance!" Brennan jogged toward her with a smile big enough to fill the forest.

In spite of the setting sun, it was now bright enough for him to see her cheeks turn pink. All Brennan had to do was glance her way and she became a melted puddle of snow. "You're too kind, your highness."

The prince looped his arm through hers. "My darling, we are engaged now. I should think you can call me by my name." He pressed a kiss to her head and Lennox swooned.

This was ridiculous. They weren't really engaged. She needed to get a handle on herself.

They joined the king and queen to watch the ceremony, and the elated feelings Lennox had upon seeing Brennan vanished under the harsh gaze of the queen.

Only a few days remained, a few days to determine what to do, and then she would no longer need to deal with the queen's judgement.

Around a giant bonfire, Priestesses of Luana danced. Their silver robes shone like a shower of falling stars. Two snow-covered hills beyond framed the perfect view of the setting sun.

The High Priestess stood on a platform and raised her arms. It looked as though she held the sun. She sang about Luana giving up her life with Ray the sun god so she could rule the night once again and restore order to the world. But every few generations, a piece of each of them would reside in the soul of their Chosens. The two would be married and able to live out their love as humans on earth, bringing the kingdoms together.

Lennox glanced at Brennan. His sapphire eyes sparkled in the fire-light, and she saw the hope and love of this tradition in them. As much as he wanted to go about things his way, maybe having his daughter be Luana's Chosen meant more to him than he let on. It made her heart swell. Their hands brushed against one another and he interlaced his fingers with hers. He met her gaze, but there was a sadness behind his smile.

If she'd said yes to his original proposal, it was possible their child could be the one to bring this legend to fruition. Lennox swallowed the lump forming in her throat. It was a lovely story.

Brennan leaned down toward her. "I have something for you."

From his pocket he pulled out a simple green band fashioned of twigs, leaves, and white roses. "I had to have a betrothal band made for you in a hurry. But it's all things found in our garden, which I thought you would like."

He slid the band over her left hand, so it wrapped around her wrist. Shimmers of stardust sprinkled over it. She turned her wrist back and forth to let the firelight catch the sparkles and make it shine. "It's beautiful. But I don't have one for you."

"Never mind that. I'm just glad you like it." He kissed her gloved knuckles. A few of the people around them who saw, sighed at the show of affection. The queen snorted.

The romantic gestures were for show, to convince everyone their engagement was real. For a moment, Lennox had let herself get swept up in the romance of Luana and Ray's legend. Which was ridiculous. She didn't even want to marry the prince, did she?

"Are you prepared for such a large role?" The queen kept her eyes on the ceremony but had the crisp tone she seemed to reserve for Lennox alone. "You'd better be who you claim, for not many would be able to shoulder such a position."

The moment was broken when a cheer burst from the crowd. As the sun set, lanterns of starlight Lennox hadn't noticed before erupted all around them, illuminating the space into a magical star-filled wonderland.

Brennan wagged his brows at Lennox. "Now the real fun begins."

Good. She needed some fun.

Brennan led her to a large field between the hills. Stands were scattered all around giving out treats and beverages and small toys to the children along with extra scarves, hats, and gloves. There were places for people to make feeders for small birds and animals and gifts for one another. At the very front stood a sign with a schedule of events, advertising everything from snow creature building, to a winter fashion show, to music, and sled races.

Lennox laughed. "This is not how I imagined nobles and royals celebrating the winter solstice."

"The fancy ball is tomorrow," Brennan answered as he tightened his scarf. "Although that one is rather fun too if I do say so myself."

They wandered through the different stands, testing the different foods and treats they had to offer. People stopped to talk and greet the prince often, and they greeted Lennox just as warmly, offering their congratulations on the engagement. Everyone was delighted at the thought of their prince finally getting married and of having a connection to Eral Forest. The love they had for Brennan was evident in their faces. It pained Lennox more and more with each person to know their hopes would be dashed when they broke off the faux relationship.

"This is nothing like I imagined it would be," she confessed as they climbed to the top of one of the hills for a sled race.

"Why do you say that?" Brennan asked. He examined the selection of sleds until he found one he liked most and pulled it out.

"Mother always said how much she hated court. The people were stuck up and too traditional and looked down on those living in Eral. But I haven't seen that at all. They're all so kind and want to know more about my life in the forest and how we can be more connected."

They walked to where the sled racers were lining up and Prince Brennan set theirs on the ground. "We aren't all that way. For a long time Eral seemed to be wild and dangerous. I used to be told scary bedtime stories of the monsters that live there. You saw how my mother reacted to you. She believes anyone out of the ordinary should be stayed away from."

How could she forget?

"But you're right, more and more people are moving away from those ideas and want us to unite, or at least be friendly toward one another." He took a seat on the sled and patted the wood slabs between his legs. "I have a place for you right here."

Heat spread to Lennox's cheeks again, and to lower places this time. From the sly smile on his face, she knew he didn't mean that phrase in an entirely innocent way. "It looks cozy."

"Very."

She lowered herself onto the wooden sled and nestled between his legs. The wood seat was cold, but she warmed as the prince pulled her in close to his chest and wrapped his arms around to reach the rope in front.

"My mother and some of the other forest dwellers have been hesitant about those who live in the kingdoms too," Lennox said in an attempt to distract herself. It didn't do much good though, as when she turned to him their faces were so close, she could see each eyelash surrounding his bright blue eyes. "Perhaps when this is all over, we can still find a way for our people to be friends."

"I'd like that."

His lips were a bright pink from the cold. It would be so easy to lean forward just a tad and kiss them. His blue eyes flickered down to her lips then back up at her eyes again. Maybe he wanted to kiss her too. She shouldn't kiss him and let herself dive too deeply into this facade.

"On your marks!"

Lennox jumped at the sound of the race announcer's harsh voice. The sled race. That's right.

"Get set!"

The pair snapped out of the trance they'd been in and readied themselves to go down the hill. Brennan planted a foot in the snow, prepared to push off.

"Go!" A horn sounded and they were off.

Lennox yelled as their sled sped down the hill, the evening wind cold against her cheeks. Silver and white stardust followed in their wake. The stardust flew from the sleds all around, illuminating the hills as though they were gliding through the galaxy itself. If the ride alone wasn't enough to take her breath away, Brennan's hard, strong body pressed behind her did the job.

They hit a bump and the sled jumped and jolted to the side. "Hold on!" Brennan yelled and directed the sled as it veered off course. It bumped and slid and jolted some more. He was able to avoid them hitting any other racers but not another bump, and they flipped out into the snow.

With a shriek Lennox landed on her back in a soft pile of snow with Brennan beside her.

"Are you all right?"

She laughed. "Amazing." She turned to see Brennan lying on his side facing her, the way he did when they were in bed together. Snow tangled in his dark hair and settled on his eyelashes. This time he was even closer. She felt his chest heaving as hard as hers. Her eyes flickered to where snow had landed on his lips. She gulped. "Are you?"

"Amazing." The word was barely out when his mouth met hers.

He pulled away and shook his head. "I'm sorry. I shouldn't have—"

"Don't be." He was right. He shouldn't have, and she shouldn't either. But there was nothing else she wanted more. She wrapped her arms around his neck and pulled him back in for another kiss. In spite of the snow, every part of her warmed, and she groaned when he pulled away a second time.

"Come with me." With a swift hop to his feet, he lended her a hand, and led her around the corner to one of the gardens. "Now we have a bit more privacy."

Lennox could only nod, her mind foggy from the cold and his lips. They collided into one another. He pressed her against a tree, his mouth wandering all the way down to her neck. It was one of the only areas not illuminated by the star lanterns, allowing them to explore and tease without anyone seeing. When his strong hand cupped her breast, she couldn't help but moan and arch into him, rubbing her body against his member growing harder with each movement.

"Brennan! Wherever did you go?"

The sound of the queen's voice stopped them cold. Brennan swore as he rested his head against her shoulder.

"She has impeccable timing," Lennox's voice was barely a whisper as she attempted to catch her breath.

Brennan chuckled. "Indeed."

He stepped away and Lennox adjusted her disheveled clothing. She was full of stupid ideas these days, but fucking the prince in the castle gardens certainly made the top of the list.

"You may need to go on without me," Brennan said. "I need to...compose myself a bit."

It was Lennox's turn to chuckle.

"Perhaps we can continue later?" He looked at her with those bright blue eyes. The same hope and longing Lennox had inside of her filled them.

She nodded. "Yes. Later."

***

By the time Lennox got back to her room and had changed into her nightgown, she still didn't have a solution to the ogres, or for finding the purpose of this stack of mattresses. She paced in front of the bed with her hands on her hips.

Murmuring another song of Eral, Lennox summoned her magic. Vines and leaves twined around her arms then journeyed to the bed. They crawled down her body then spread across the room and up the mattresses. A soft green glow surrounded them, and Lennox's veins danced.

A knock came at the door, and Brennan poked his head around it. "May I come in?" Awe glazed his eyes as he took in the sight of her vines covering the mattresses. "Incredible."

"I'm trying to figure out what I'm supposed to do with this bed."

He raised a brow. "I could think of a few things."

She nudged him with her elbow, even though heat spread through her at the thought of what they could do in said bed. "What your mother wants me to do with it."

"Oh, yes. I'm sure she and I have entirely different ideas."

He circled around the bed, inspecting it the way Lennox had. "Any thoughts?"

She followed his path and shook her head. "There's an item I think, something small. I'm going to leave the vines today and give them time to search the bed."

The pair found their way back around to the ladder and climbed to the top, the vines and leaves still glowing around them. Side by side they lay on the bed facing one another.

"Did you enjoy the night?" he asked.

"I did, more than I thought I would," Lennox answered. She couldn't remember the last time she felt so happy and excited. It made her heart sink to think of having to disappoint them all when she didn't marry Brennan.

He tucked a stray strand of red hair behind her ear, making her shiver. "I'm glad."

There was a sort of silent intimacy now between them. It was natural when he welcomed her into his arms, and she pressed her head against his chest to talk about the events of the night. Then, when he cupped her face in his palms and kissed her, it didn't overwhelm her, but was as natural as breathing. This was beyond a stupid idea now. It had become idiotic. Reckless. Lennox didn't care as they rubbed and explored each other over their clothing. It may have only been a temporary situation, but she wanted to take advantage of every moment.

"How is it that I feel like I already know you?" he asked as he kissed her earlobe.

"I'm not sure, but I feel the same."

"But I want to know you more." His kisses trailed down her jawline until he came to her neck and sucked on the sensitive place near her collar, all the while palming her breast. His thumb found her nipple beneath the fabric of her nightgown.

She gasped. "Let me show you."

She needed him to see her, to know her, and when he leaned back, she gripped the nightgown and inched the skirt up her body. It slid over her, and she reveled at his groan when her wet womanhood was revealed, and then, again, at her breasts, nipples pink, firm and ready for him.

"Gods you're perfect." He leaned over, ready to take her, but she placed her palms on his broad chest.

"I want to know you as well."

With a sly smile Lennox wanted to kiss, he followed suit and peeled off his clothing. The purple robe fell away first, revealing the muscled chest she'd lusted after the entirety of the day before, then the loose-fitting pants, which to her delight had nothing underneath. Only a strong stiff cock she'd been imagining all night.

They collided into one another, a tangle of lips and limbs, skin to skin. When his hand slid between them and rubbed Lennox between her legs she moaned and ground her hips.

"So wet already," he said and slid a pair of fingers inside.

She could barely respond as he prepared her for him, making her shake and grasp onto him. "Fuck me. Please."

"No need to ask me twice." His fingers left her body, leaving her empty and wanting, then he kissed her as she spread her legs.

He kissed each breast and then her sensitive and throbbing clit before rising back up, grasping his cock and sliding it inside of her. He fit so tight and perfect, she moaned and wrapped her legs around his waist. It didn't take long before they moved in sync with one another, and Lennox was screaming for more. She'd never had such a connection with a partner before. Their bodies fit together perfectly, and she wanted nothing more than let him fuck her for as long as either of them could go. When they each came with cries of joy, she knew she would need to make this charade last as long as possible.

5

Lennox's back ached the next morning. She wished it was because of her and Brennans activities. But it wasn't. When they'd finally decided to go to sleep, she had been unable to get comfortable.

Brennan rolled over and his brows furrowed when he saw her rubbing her back. "Did you sleep all right?"

"No. Didn't you feel that?"

He shook his head. "Feel what?"

She groaned and lay back against the pillows. "It was as though something poked at the small of my back for hours. I barely slept. Like a tiny ball of hail, or a stone." She climbed over him to get to the ladder. "It's got to be whatever your mother planted in the bed."

He leaned over to watch her descent. "But you didn't feel it before."

The first day she'd been so exhausted and entranced by how she was sleeping next to a prince she wouldn't have noticed if a dragon had burst into the room. This time, she had her vines wrapped around the bed, sensing it for her. With one hand she held onto the ladder and the other ran across the edges of the mattresses. She reached out with her magic to sense whatever was wedged in there. Toward the middle of the pile, the glow brightened. It was as though something was pulling her hand toward it.

She closed her eyes and focused on the vines, letting her mind and body relax as they pushed between the mattresses. The weight of all of the mattresses on top made it difficult for the vines to squeeze through, but they slivered into the bed like a snake in search of its next meal. The pull grew stronger as they slid and searched until they hit a tiny bump. A shiver ran through Lennox.

There it was.

One vine wrapped itself around the object and she guided it out of the bed. She finally opened her eyes and her palm where the vine placed a tiny, green pea.

"What is it?" Brennan called from on top of the bed.

"A pea."

A damned little pea to prove she was Renata's daughter.

"A what?"

A pea? A pea was the thing in the way of being worthy of marrying the prince.

Fuming, Lennox made the rest of the way down the ladder to make room for Brennan to join her on the floor. When he stood next to her, she held out her palm. He stared at the pea as though it was the most wondrous thing he'd ever beheld.

"My mother has gone mad."

Lennox clutched the minuscule vegetable in a fist, careful to not crush it, and stormed to the vanity where her robe lay over the stool. She shoved her arms through it to cover her still naked body as though she were punching an ogre. "Where is she?"

Brennan's eyes grew wide. "My mother? Now?"

"Yes. I'm sure she's awake."

Blinded by fury, she charged through the bedroom door in search of the queen. Vines trailed in her wake and leaves flurried around her head.

"She'll be in the great hall, but maybe we should dress first," Brennan called, his bare feet slapping on the stone floor as he chased after her.

The great hall. Good. She had a direction.

When Lennox arrived, she pushed the doors open and charged inside, prepared to give the queen a piece of her mind about the pea. But she stopped dead in her tracks unprepared for who stood before her.

"Mama."

Mama with her long and wild hair, more gray than red these days, stood next to the Queen of Cresin in her patched-up dress as though she were just as elegant and regal.

"Hello darling."

Brennan ran in after her, clutching the blanket he wore around his waist. He stopped cold. "Oh, my."

The queen heaved a sigh. "At least your child bothered to wear some semblance of clothing."

"What are you doing here, Mama?"

Mama stalked toward her then stopped, placing the end of her wooden staff on the ground, making it echo through the room. "When I found out my daughter was engaged, I thought it only appropriate I come and meet my future in-laws for their grand Winter Solstice Ball."

Lennox and Brennan glanced at one another with panicked looks. She hadn't planned on having to keep up the facade around Mama.

"I..."

Brennan leaned in closer to her. "Lennox, maybe we should come out with it. With her here, we can protect both of you and make a plan."

She gaped at him and her heart dropped. Of course, that had been the plan all along, but it felt so soon. And after everything... "Is that what you want?"

Mama waved her off. "Never mind that now. We have bigger problems to solve. The ogre is coming."

"What?" Lennox and Brennan asked in unison.

"I thought you said you wouldn't bring them here," the queen snapped at her.

"She didn't. I did," Mama corrected. "They were also surprised at the news of your engagement and followed me."

The room shook again and there stood a green, fanged ogre who took up half of the doorway. He was the one who'd been after Lennox all this time. He snarled at the group and his muscles bulged against his fur and leather vest. "Give me my bride."

Brennan stepped in front of Lennox as though he were going to take this ogre down himself, clad only in a blanket.

This was ridiculous. She was the daughter of Kutlaous' Minister and the fiancé—albeit pretend—of the prince of Cresin. She would not be bullied by an ogre. No one was going to tell her how to live her life, not this ogre, not Mama, and not even Brennan. He suggested marrying her in the first place, and when things got difficult, he suggested backing out of their plan? Didn't she get any say at all?

She pursed her lips and clutched the pea in her palm. She had an idea but would need help.

"Mama, take my hand." She outstretched her arm and showed Mother the pea.

"Darling, a pea?"

The ogre growled again and slammed his club in his palm. "No more of these games! I will have my bride!"

Mama took Lennox's hand, and Lennox summoned her magic. After a moment, she could feel Mama's joining in with her. The pea trembled and shook in their palms and from between their fingers vines and more peas poured out toward the ogre. Brennan leaped out of the way as the vines slithered and crawled toward their target. The ogre pounded at them with his club and jumped around the room, but between Lennox and Renata it was no use. Their magic was more powerful and faster than he was. The vines wrapped around the ogre, tripping him as he tried to break free.

He fell to the floor with a thud and the vines continued to wrap him in a perfect pod.

Lennox breathed a sigh of relief as she let go of Mama's hand. She turned on her heel and went to the queen, then presented the pea. "I imagine this is what I had to find in order to prove myself?"

For the first time, the queen had a genuine smile for Lennox. "I knew you'd find it. Only a true daughter of Eral Forest would be able to sense such a small piece of nature and use it in such a way."

Lennox's shoulders fell. "What do you mean 'use it in such a way'?"

The queen offered a small shrug and gestured to the ogre. "I was actually the one who led him here. If your story was true, I knew he would be angry, and I wanted to be sure you could handle the situation. If my son is to marry you, you need to be someone who can hold her own."

Brennan stepped forward, still clinging to the blanket around his waist for dear life. "Wait. Mother, you brought this ogre here and endangered everyone?"

The queen rolled her eyes. "I had plenty of guards on standby in case things went awry. We were always perfectly safe."

"Unbelievable." Brennan shook his head.

They stood there in the grand room in silence. What had just happened?

"Well," Mama said bringing them all back to focus. "The ball is to start soon, and I'd imagine you don't want an ogre here for it. Besides... clothes would probably be recommended."

6

The ball room was even grander than when Lennox arrived two nights ago. Not only did greenery and flowers lay all around, but stardust floated through the air, and a large tree stood in the center decorated in stars and ribbons.

Lennox glided down the steps and across the dance floor in her green gown, the shade of a frosted pine tree, as she searched for Prince Brennan. It made her feel regal and elegant - queenly even. He stood in the middle of the room surrounded by people, but when he saw her, he stepped away and took her hand to kiss it.

"You look stunning."

"So do you." He did, in his dark gray jacket and silver sash, his sapphire eyes shining. "We need to talk."

They danced and swirled into the crowd the way they had that first night when he'd suggested they marry. It was hardly something one would call a proper proposal, but it was a proposal. "When you suggested earlier that we tell Mama the truth, is that what you truly wanted, and thought was best?"

"You were the one who turned me down originally," Brennan pointed out. "I thought you wanted to resolve your ogre issue and move on. You said it would be easiest."

He had her there. It was his idea for the engagement, but when she resisted, he'd amended it to a fake relationship. "Well, yes. I suppose it ending so soon surprised me."

His grip around her waist tightened and a quirk came to his lips. "How long were you expecting us to go on?"

"The situation with the ogre isn't entirely resolved. He might be captured, but you never know if he'll come searching for me again. I think we should continue for a few more days... perhaps even weeks." Gods, she was babbling. She should have prepared what she wanted to say better, but there hadn't been much time.

Little by little her chest pressed against his and their movements slowed. Still dancing, but barely. "If that is the case, perhaps I should stop pretending I haven't been in love with you since I first saw you at the castle gate, frozen to the bone."

It was as though everything, including the beating of Lennox's heart, stopped. "You have?"

"I have."

"I'm in love with you too." She could hardly believe she said out loud what she'd been thinking and feeling these last couple of days, while convincing herself it was impossible to fall in love with someone so quickly. But as she did, she knew it with her whole heart to be true.

Brennan stopped their dancing and held her face in his hands for a deep kiss that left her spinning. "I suppose that settles that."

Lennox couldn't hold back her smile. "I suppose so."

"You know this means you cannot live in Eral Forest."

She nodded. "I know. Mama will be furious, but I don't want to leave you, or the people of Cresin. And it won't be easy. We still hardly know one another, and there will be resistance from some. It has been easy so far, but there's going to come a time, I don't know when, but you'll have to resist the traditions and ways of your people. I need to know that you'll be there when it happens."

For a moment the smile was gone from Brennan's face, but there was no lack of love in his eyes. "How do you know?"

"You'll be king. It's never easy."

He leaned down and kissed her forehead. "If you're by my side, I'll be able to do anything."

They spun in circles and danced around the shimmering tree, the glitter of the stardust glimmering on their clothes and across the ball-room floor.

"This is a stupid idea, isn't it?" Lennox asked him.

"Maybe. But those are my favorite."

"Mine too."

Farren Castle's Winter Solstice Punch

- Apple Cider
- Cranberry Juice
- Fresh Cranberries
- Pomegranate Seeds
- Orange
- Cinnamon Stick
- Dash of Ground Clove
- Dash of Ground Nutmeg
- Dash of Ground Cinnamon
- Rum

1. Mix and cook the punch together either on the stove in a large pot, or in a slow cooker on low heat.
2. Use a 2:1 ratio, 2 parts cider to 1 part cranberry juice. Quantities will depend on how many you're serving, but for 4 drinks use 4 cups cider and 2 cups cranberry juice
3. Put a few good handfuls of cranberries and pomegranate seeds in
4. Add three cinnamon sticks
5. Slice the orange and squeeze it a little bit before you put it in the pot
6. Sprinkle the spices in

7. Stir and bring to a simmer over medium heat and cook for
   about 10 minutes or keep slow cooker on low until heated
8. Serve in mugs and spike with as much rum as desired

Appendix

A GUIDE TO THE DEITIES

Luana, goddess of the moon
Other influences: stars, darkness, winter, ice, night
Color: Blue
Common Symbols: Moon in various stages, stars, snowflakes
High Temple Location: Farren Castle in Cresin
Appearance: Slender woman with long dark hair and pale skin

Ray, god of the sun
Other influences: clouds, light, summer, fire, day
Color: Yellow
Common Symbols: Sun, fire, sand, cloud, phoenix, dragon
High Temple Location: Cyre Palace—the Golden Palace—in Oxare
Appearance: Large, muscular man with golden skin and flaming hair

Kutlaous, god of nature
Other influences: forest, jungle, agriculture, animals, plants
Color: Green
Common Symbols: Vine, stag, horns, leaves, flowers, animals
High Temple Location: Eral Forest
Appearance: Human man with horns on his head and hooves for
feet, green skin with vines wrapped around his body

Aros, god of war
Other influences: hunting, fitness, athletes
Color: Red
Common Symbols: sword, arrow, snake, lion

High Temple Location: Khadi Desert
Appearance: Tall, almost giant man with white skin, red eyes, and shaved head

Colma, god of water
Other influences: water creatures, other liquids, drinks
Color: Blue or green
Common Symbols: waves, fish, pitcher, ship, mermaid tail
High Temple Location: Dravian Islands
Appearance: Lanky yet muscular man with translucent skin, long blue hair, often wearing blue robes

Stula, goddess of death
Other influences: sickness, disability, change, maturity
Color: Purple
Common Symbols: skull, bones, rose, clock, raven
High Temple Location: Underworld
Appearance: Woman with dark skin, purple hair, and black robes

Yla, deity of birth
Other influences: fertility, childhood
Color: Pink
Common Symbols: Footprints, lotus flower, baby animals, egg
High Temple Location: Oxare Coast
Appearance: No one knows their "true" appearance, as they come as they are needed. A middle-aged woman to be a midwife; a young man preparing for fatherhood; a pregnant woman; a grandparent, etc. The commonalities are brown hair and a tattoo of the lotus flower.

Diar, deity of love
Other influences: Beauty, desire, charity
Color: Red or Pink
Common Symbols: rose, heart, ribbons intertwined or tied together,

doves
High Temple Location: Belovian Islands
Appearance: A nonbinary being containing anatomy of both male
and female, long and flowing pink hair and light-brown skin

Efarae, goddess of inspiration
Other influences: the arts, keepers of the deities' tales
Color: Lavender
Common Symbols: music notes, a quill, paint brush, owl, scroll
High Temple Location: Kingdom of Marali
Appearance: Petite woman with blonde hair, purple eyes, and
often wearing glasses

Gallis, goddess of restoration
Other influences: healing, health, fitness, building
Color: Gold
Common Symbols: a chalice, building tools, bandages, tonic
bottles, hands
High Temple Location: Kingdom of Imare
Appearance: A round and plump yet strong woman with brown
hair and golden robes

Acknowledgements

This short story was so much fun to write! I adore the holiday season, and I'm so glad this little prequel can have life.

The first thanks goes to God for giving me so many opportunities and being the original author and artist. I would be no where without his love and grace.

Thank you to the Tina Moss and Yelena Casale and the whole City Owl team! You all believed in me and this series. Without City Owl Press, The Cursed Queens wouldn't exist. I'm so proud to be an Owl and to have the privilege to work with such an amazing team and alongside such talented authors.

Thank you, Laura Cox for this amazing cover and for formatting this story. Your work is so gorgeous, and I've always dreamed of having my own cover that you've created. Thank you for being such a wonderful friend and taking up this little project!

Thank you to Natalie, Tim, Elsie, and Patrick. Your love and support mean more than you know. (Even if the kids are a little young to be reading this.)

Thank you, Mom and Dad for supporting all my wild ideas and being my rocks.

Thank you, Dale for the hours of listening to me talk about ideas, covers, insecurities, joys, and woes. I'm so grateful every day that you understand this writing life and are going through it right there with me.

And finally, thank you to my readers! All of this is for you. Thank you for all the support, shares, reviews, likes, comments, and encouragement. You're the ones who have truly given these books wings and I keep going for you.

E.E. Hornburg is a Chicago South-sider, consumer of nachos, dog mom, aunt to the greatest niece ever, and owner of far too many mugs and travel cups which hold her coffee. When not creating or devouring books you can find her belting show tunes, playing with her dog and niece and nephew, and plotting how she can get to Disney World (again). Hornburg is the author of the Cursed Queens series. The first two books, The Night's Chosen and The Shadow's Heir are available now, and The Forest's Keeper will be available in the spring of 2023. Her first Kindle Vella story, Ebeneezer & Marley is now available with new episodes releasing every Wednesday leading up to Christmas 2022.

You can receive all of her updates and free stories by signing up for her newsletter at www.emilyhornburg.com.

www.ingramcontent.com/pod-product-compliance
Lightning Source LLC
Chambersburg PA
CBHW071234140726
47996CB00007B/2594